SHAWN and KEEPER

Show-and-Tell

by Jonathan London

illustrated by Renée Williams-Andriani

PUFFIN BOOKS

For Sean and Keeper, and Xavier too—J.L.

To Maggie, Ellen, and Joseph—R.W.-A.

PUFFIN BOOKS
Published by the Penguin Group
Penguin Putnam Books for Young Readers, 345 Hudson Street, New York, New York 10014, U.S.A.
Penguin Books Ltd, 27 Wrights Lane, London W8 5TZ, England
Penguin Books Australia Ltd, Ringwood, Victoria, Australia
Penguin Books Canada Ltd, 10 Alcorn Avenue, Toronto, Ontario, Canada M4V 3B2
Penguin Books (N.Z.) Ltd, 182-190 Wairau Road, Auckland 10, New Zealand

Penguin Books Ltd, Registered Offices: Harmondsworth, Middlesex, England

First published in the United States of America by Dutton Children's Books and Puffin Books,
members of Penguin Putnam Books for Young Readers, 2000

1 3 5 7 9 10 8 6 4 2

Text copyright © Jonathan London, 2000
Illustrations copyright © Renée Williams-Andriani, 2000
All rights reserved

Puffin Books ISBN 0-14-130367-0
Puffin® and Easy-to-Read® are registered trademarks of Penguin Putnam Inc.

Printed in Hong Kong
Set in ITC Century Book

Reading Level 1.6

Shawn and Keeper

did everything together.

They were the best of friends.

They walked together
and talked together.

They growled together
and howled together.

They ate together

and cleaned the plate together.

One day, Shawn said,

"Mom, I want to take Keeper

to show-and-tell on Friday!

We'll do tricks together."

"Good idea," said Mom.

On Monday, Shawn trained

Keeper to sit.

"Good boy!" Shawn said.

He gave Keeper a cookie.

On Tuesday, Shawn trained
Keeper to lie down.

"Good boy!" Shawn said.
He gave Keeper a cookie.

On Wednesday and Thursday,

Shawn trained Keeper

to shake hands and fetch.

"Good boy!" Shawn said.

He gave Keeper a cookie.

"Oh, I love you so much!" said Shawn.

"Woof!" barked Keeper.

Finally, it was Friday.

It was time for show-and-tell!

First, Leah sang to her mouse.

Then Max showed his
pet snake.

And Emma did a hat trick

with her rabbit.

"And now," said the teacher,

"Shawn's dog, Keeper,

will do some tricks!"

"Sit!" said Shawn.

But Keeper stood up.

He wagged his tail.

He licked Shawn's face.

"Lie down!" said Shawn.

But Keeper scratched his ear.

He sniffed the air.

He sniffed the teacher.

"Shake hands!" said Shawn.

But Keeper lay down

and rolled over.

All the kids scratched his belly.

"Fetch!" said Shawn.

But Keeper tripped the teacher.

He jumped over a desk.

He spilled cups of pencils

and bottles of glue.

He sent papers flying . . .

and knocked over the fish tank—

splash!

"Oh no!" cried Shawn.

When Shawn caught Keeper,

he said, "Bad boy!

But I still love you."

And he gave Keeper a cookie.

After school,

Shawn and Keeper walked together

and talked together.

They growled together

and howled together.

They were the best of friends.